Published in English in Canada and the USA in 2021 by
Groundwood Books
Text and illustrations copyright © 2018 by Isol
Translation copyright © 2021 by Elisa Amado

Groundwood Books / House of Anansi Press
groundwoodbooks.com

Groundwood Books respectfully acknowledges that the land on
which we operate is the Traditional Territory of many Nations,
including the Anishinabeg, the Wendat, and the Haudenosaunee.
It is also the Treaty Lands of the Mississaugas of the Credit.

We gratefully acknowledge the Government of Canada for its
financial support of our publishing program.

With the participation of the Government of Canada
Avec la participation du gouvernement du Canada | Canadä

Library and Archives Canada Cataloguing in Publication
Title: Impossible / Isol.
Other titles: Imposible. English
Names: Isol, author, illustrator. | Amado, Elisa, translator.
Description: Translation of: Imposible. | Translated by Elisa Amado.
Identifiers: Canadiana (print) 20200276522 | Canadiana (ebook)
20200276530 | ISBN 9781773064345 (hardcover) | ISBN
9781773064352 (EPUB) | ISBN 9781773064369 (Kindle)
Classification: LCC PZ7.I86 Imp 2021 | DDC j863/.64—dc23

The art has been created using charcoal, ink and digital collage.
Printed and bound in Malaysia

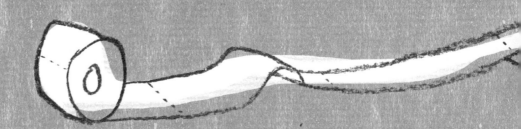

ISOL

IMPOSSIBLE

Translated by Elisa Amado

GROUNDWOOD BOOKS

HOUSE OF ANANSI PRESS

TORONTO / BERKELEY

Toribio is two and a half

and his parents love him
very much.

But they would also love to
get some sleep.

"Your turn," says Dad.

"But I went last time," says Mom.

His parents would love
to have more peaceful
days as well.

"What happened?"

Eating without a fuss would be nice.

"Sure you don't want to go to the bathroom?"

"Suuuuure."

They'd be very pleased if Toribio would only try the beautiful potty they just bought him.

By evening his parents are exhausted.

And they dream of a time when Toribio might change

and everything would be much easier.

Then one day, they see an encouraging ad in the paper:
"Tired? Worried? Mrs. Meridien can solve any problem — family, health, money, love. Scientific method. Natural remedies. Fast results."

They ask for an appointment immediately.

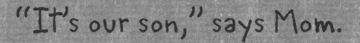

"Good afternoon," says the specialist. "What can I do for you?"

"It's our son," says Mom.

"We want Toribio to change," says Dad. "But it seems impossible."

Toribio's exhausted parents
follow the instructions and
sleep all through the night.

They sleep so long that it is daytime when they wake up.

"Wow! Can it be that Toribio is still asleep?"

"Do you think he's all right?"

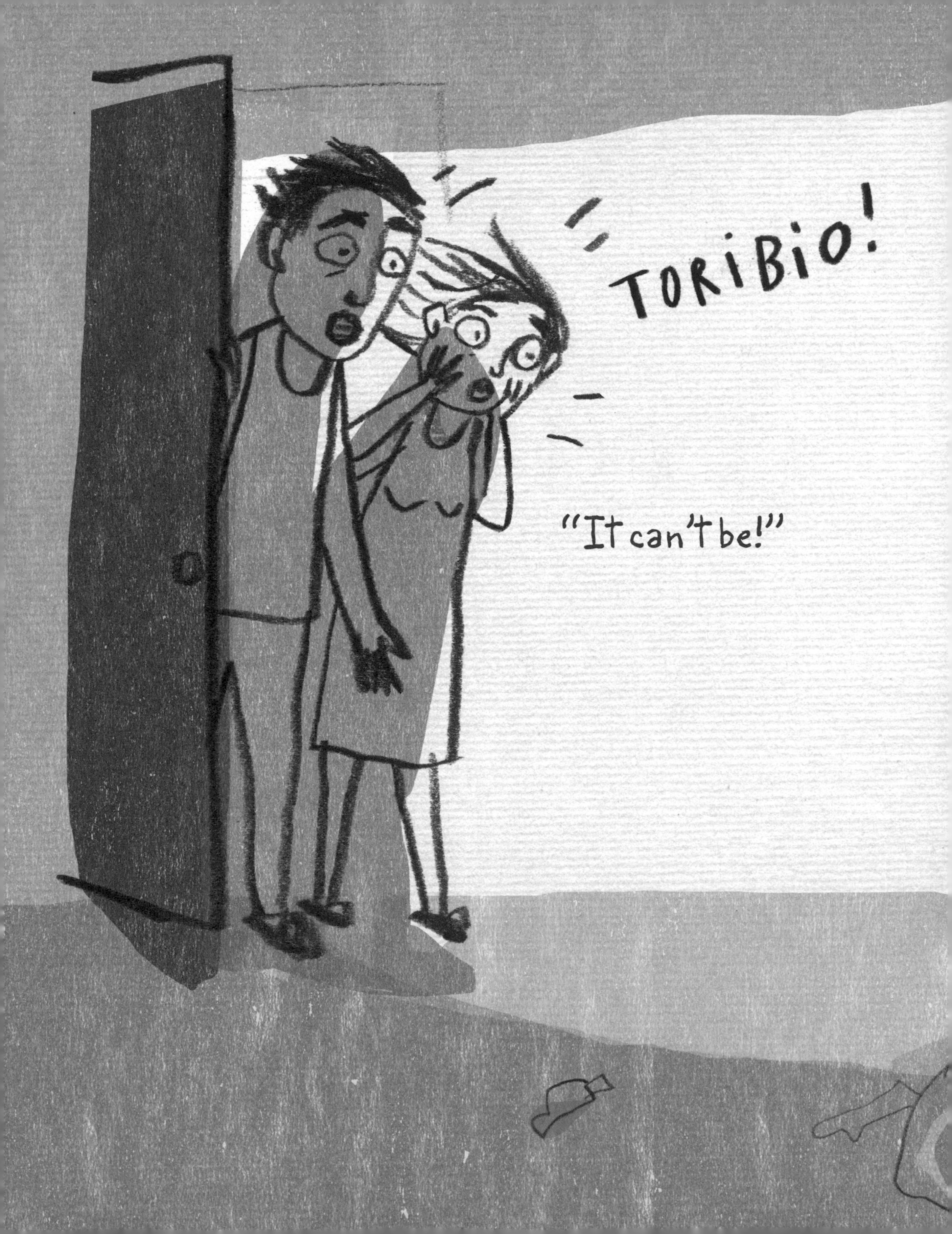
TORIBIO!
"It can't be!"

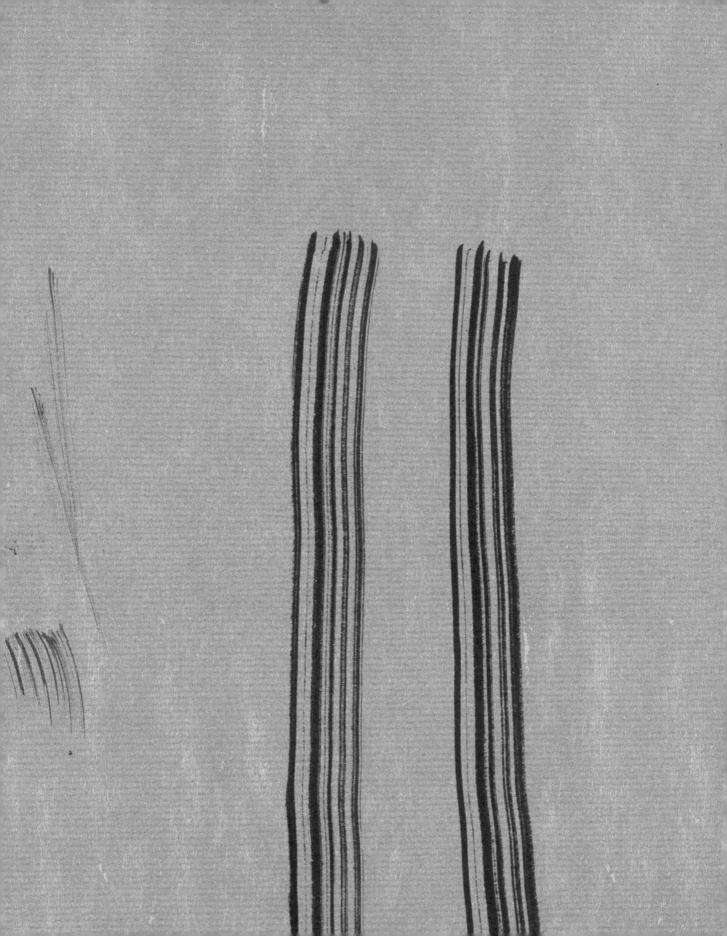